WE FOUND A SITE!

IT'S NOT PRETTY...

...BUT IT WILL DO THE TRICK.

WHAT HAPPENED TO YOUR HAIR?

FORTUNE SMILED UPON HIM.

OKAY, KIDS. YOU'VE FOUND A SITE. BUT NOW WE NEED TO TALK ABOUT WHAT COMES NEXT.

YOU'RE GOING TO NEED—

MONEY! WE KNOW!

YES. YOU SEE, THERE ARE MANY FACTORS TO CONSIDER WHEN BUILDING A SKATE PARK. YOU'RE GOING TO NEED—

I'VE GOT THREE DOLLARS.

I THINK I'VE GOT SEVEN...

MAKE THAT FOUR.

BOUNSKI HAS FIFTEEN.

YOU'RE GOING TO NEED A LOT MORE THAN FORTY-SIX DOLLARS AND EIGHTY-SIX CENTS TO BUILD A SKATE PARK.

IT COULD COST AS MUCH AS A MILLION DOLLARS.

SHORTY?!

I'M OKAY.

I'M OKAY.

LOOK GUYS. JUST BECAUSE YOU DON'T HAVE THE MONEY NOW DOESN'T MEAN YOU CAN'T GET IT AT ALL.

BUT WHERE ARE WE GOING TO GET SO MUCH?

FROM YOUR INGENUITY, PINKY. ALL YOU HAVE TO DO IS BELIEVE IN YOURSELVES.

HERE, VISIT THE DEPARTMENT OF PARKS AND RECREATION. ASK FOR STACIE DUMONT.

I'LL TELL HER YOU'RE COMING. SHE'LL BE ABLE TO HELP YOU WITH WHAT COMES NEXT.

STACIE DUMONT

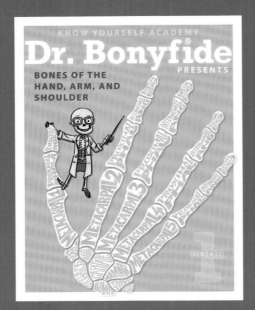

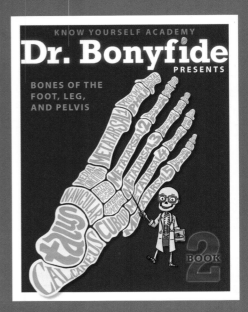

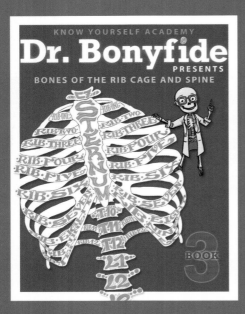

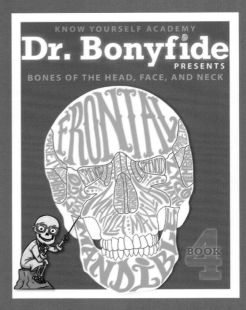

Join Dr. Bonyfide and Pinky on a journey to the inside of you!
It's knowledge to last a lifetime.
Get your copies at

KN WYOURSELF.COM

In Book 3, Vinnie Vertebrae guides Pinky through the spine and rib cage, where she learns to stand tall and keep her head up.

Join Dr. Bonyfide and Pinky on a journey to the inside of you! Get your copies at

KNOWYOURSELF.COM

ENTER THIS PORTAL FOR
ADVENTURE 4
TIME SKATERS

You've Got
to be Kidney

I AM HOPING THE CHANGE IN THE AMBER IS AN INDICATION WE ARE GETTING CLOSER TO FINDING DR. B.

DOES THAT MEAN WHAT I THINK IT MEANS?

GRAB THE HISTORATOR!

SAFE VOYAGE, YOU TWO!

YOU *TWO??*

HANG ON, NEWBIE!

AAAAAAA!!!!!

WHAT DO WE DO?

HAAAANK!!

YES, YES, WHAT IS IT?

OH!

RUN TOWARDS THAT PORTAL!

MY APOLOGIES, LADIES...

THAT WAS THE NILE RIVER I TRANSPORTED YOU TO, NOT THE EUPHRATES. SIMPLE MISCALCULATION ON MY PART.

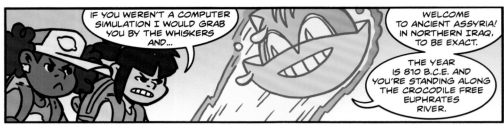

IF YOU WEREN'T A COMPUTER SIMULATION I WOULD GRAB YOU BY THE WHISKERS AND...

WELCOME TO ANCIENT ASSYRIA! IN NORTHERN IRAQ, TO BE EXACT.

THE YEAR IS 810 B.C.E. AND YOU'RE STANDING ALONG THE CROCODILE FREE EUPHRATES RIVER.

DOESN'T SEEM LIKE MUCH OF A RIVER RIGHT NOW.

HMM... ANALYSIS OF POLLEN AND CHARCOAL LEVELS INDICATE A DROUGHT HERE DURING THIS TIME.

THE EUPHRATES IS THE LONGEST RIVER IN WESTERN ASIA, AND ITS RESOURCES FLOW INTO MANY MODERN DAY COUNTRIES.

IT LITERALLY FEEDS THIS ENTIRE REGION. PEOPLE USE THE WATER FOR GROWING CROPS, FISHING, AND TRAVELING.

IT'S GONNA BE TOUGH GETTING AROUND HERE TO FIND DR. B.

NO SKATING IN THE DESERT!

IT'S WALKABLE, ABOUT HALF A MILE AWAY.

THOUGH YOU MIGHT GET SOME SAND IN YOUR SHOES.

THESE VAGRANTS WERE STEALING WATER FROM THE RIVER.

EVERYONE IN THIS LAND KNOWS THAT CLEAN WATER HAS BECOME SCARCE.

SO WHY WERE YOU BREAKING THE LAW?

WE DIDN'T KNOW... THERE WAS A LAW.

YOUR MAJESTY! PLEASE! WE'RE NOT VAGRANTS. WE'RE LOOKING FOR OUR FRIEND!

IT'S SO HOT.

A LIKELY STORY.

HONESTLY! WE DIDN'T KNOW WE COULDN'T TOUCH THE WATER.

THOUGH YOU MUST BE BRAVE YOUNG WOMEN TO VENTURE ON YOUR OWN.

GUARDS, LOWER YOUR WEAPONS.

SHORTY... WHAT HAPPENED? ARE YOU OK?

EL-BIDNAM, WHY WERE THESE TWO YOUNG GIRLS BROUGHT HERE?

CLEARLY THEY MEANT NO HARM.

THAT MAY BE SO, BUT THEY STILL BROKE THE LAW. SINCE THE WATER SUPPLY IS UNDER OUR CONTROL, IT'S IMPORTANT WE REINFORCE THE RULES.

PUNISHING THESE CHILDREN WILL DO NOTHING BUT CAUSE MORE PANIC AND FEAR.

HAVE THE SERVANTS PREPARE CHAMBERS FOR THEM. I'D LIKE THEM TO STAY AT THE PALACE AS MY GUESTS.

AS YOU WISH, YOUR HIGHNESS.

CAN YOU BELIEVE IT? YOU HAVE TO PAY TO USE THE WATER HERE.

HOW DID YOU HEAR THAT?

SOMETHING'S NOT RIGHT. HANK?

MY SCANNERS ARE SHOWING THE EUPHRATES IS FULL OF POLLUTANTS. SO WHILE THERE IS WATER, THERE IS A SHORTAGE OF CLEAN WATER.

YOUR MAJESTY, HUMANS NEED WATER TO LIVE. YOU COULD LIVE FOR A WHILE WITHOUT FOOD BUT ONLY 3 DAYS WITHOUT WATER!

THESE ORGANS CLEAN YOUR BLOODSTREAM, LIKE A FILTER. BUT THEY NEED WATER TO DO IT.

FRUIT NECTARS ARE LIQUID, BUT THEY DON'T HYDRATE THE BODY AS MUCH AS WATER DOES.

THIS IS A GIFT FROM THE GODS, INDEED. NOTHING IS MORE SACRED THAN KNOWLEDGE.

YOU MUST GET ME ONE OF MY OWN.

I'LL SEE WHAT I CAN DO...

SK'TTER...

HUH?

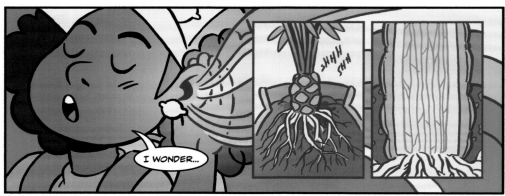

AND LET LOOSE THE WATERS OF THE EUPHRATES...

WATER WILL FLOW FREE AGAIN FOR ALL!

YOUR HIGHNESS...

DELICIOUS!

I THOUGHT YOU MIGHT WANT IT BACK.

THE FIRE AMBER FROM MY BRONZE CUFF!

THIS WAS A GIFT FROM A FRIEND. A STRANGER THAT PASSED THROUGH HERE, A BONE MAN.

A BONE MAN?

PERHAPS IT CAME TO YOU FOR A REASON.

I'D LIKE YOU TO KEEP IT.

DR. B... HE WAS HERE.

MAYBE IT'S THE SAME THING. BY HELPING OTHER PEOPLE, WE ALSO HELP OURSELVES.

THE BONE MAN SAID YOU'D COME LOOKING FOR HIM, AND THAT YOU MIGHT NEED MY HELP.

HE DIDN'T MENTION HOW MUCH I'D NEED YOUR HELP, THOUGH.

I WILL RELY ON SCIENCE AND INGENUITY TO MAKE THIS REGION THE GREATEST IN THE WORLD.

NOT IF I HAVE ANYTHING TO DO WITH IT!

GIVE ME THAT!

THAT'S MY AMBER! YOU CHILDREN HAVE NO CONCEPT OF THE POWER IT POSSESSES.

EL-BIDNAM! BUT I THOUGHT— ANOTHER BONE MAN?

GUARDS! SEIZE HIM!

QUICK, PINKY!

NOOOO!

GOOD LUCK, YOUNG GIRLS.

AND THANK YOU.

In Book 3, Ruby Rib teaches Pinky about the rigid ribs
and flexible cartilage that help the rib cage protect the heart.

Join Dr. Bonyfide and Pinky on a journey to the inside of you!
Get your copies at

In Book 4, Maxilla Gorilla takes Pinky on a jaw-dropping adventure through the skull.

Join Dr. Bonyfide and Pinky on a journey to the inside of you!
Get your copies at

KNOWYOURSELF.COM

The **RENAL** SYSTEM:
A River Runs **Through Us**

About 60% of your body is water – you are more water than you are solid! You have water inside your cells (the building blocks of your body), water in your tissues, and water in your blood. All of this water helps your body stay at the right temperature, move nutrients where they need to go, keep your moving parts from getting stuck together, and get rid of waste. To put it simply, your body needs water to survive.

Water is your most essential nutrient, but you can lose up to 2 liters a day through sweating, breathing, and getting rid of wastes in the form of urine (often known as "pee") and feces (often known as "poop"). It's very important that you drink water to replace what you lose. Your body also does not want to have too much water, so it has ways to keep the right balance. Keeping your body's systems stable is called homeostasis*.

* Say it like this:

"home-ee-oh-**stay**-sis"

Homeostasis: Embrace This!

Your body has a very important way of keeping your water in homeostasis – this is where your renal* system comes in. Renal means "having to do with the kidneys." You might know that you have 2 kidneys and that they are super important because they make urine. So they help you keep the water you need, while getting rid of the water and the wastes that you don't! Getting rid of wastes is called excretion*. The kidneys work with some other big structures in the renal system to do this.

Your kidneys are found on either side of your spine, just between your lowest ribs. Each kidney is a little smaller than your fist.

*Say it like this:

"ree-null"
"ex-cree-shun"

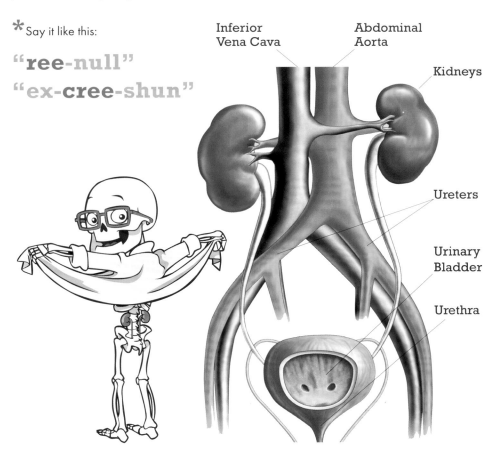

Inferior Vena Cava

Abdominal Aorta

Kidneys

Ureters

Urinary Bladder

Urethra

Your kidneys also help keep your blood cells in homeostasis. When your body needs more blood cells, your kidneys make a chemical that tells your bone marrow to produce more.

Kidneys: Your Filtration Station

Each kidney has large blood vessels that move blood into and out of it, and a ureter that carries the final waste – urine – out to the urinary bladder. The kidneys also have a lot of small blood vessels traveling through them because they filter wastes out of the blood (while keeping the good stuff like your blood cells). Your kidneys are always busy cleaning your blood. They can cleanse all the blood in your body in about 50 minutes.

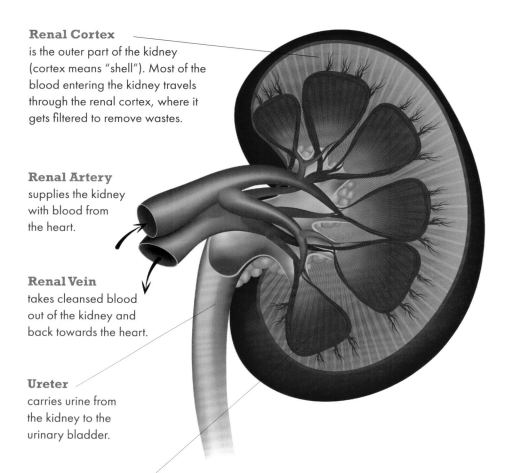

Renal Cortex
is the outer part of the kidney (cortex means "shell"). Most of the blood entering the kidney travels through the renal cortex, where it gets filtered to remove wastes.

Renal Artery
supplies the kidney with blood from the heart.

Renal Vein
takes cleansed blood out of the kidney and back towards the heart.

Ureter
carries urine from the kidney to the urinary bladder.

Renal Pyramids
are structures in the kidney medulla (the center of an organ) that contain millions of tubes that form and collect urine. This is where the kidney reabsorbs (takes back into the bloodstream) nutrients, certain chemicals, and water that the body wants to keep. Each kidney contains 5 to 11 renal pyramids, and about 1 million tube units.

Renal Pyramid: The Journey Within

Let's zoom in on a section of a renal pyramid and the layer of cortex above it. The working units of the kidney are made up of loops of tubes called nephrons* and larger tubes called collecting ducts. Each kidney has about 1 million of these units.

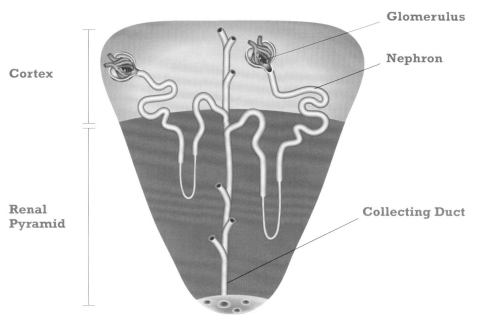

Cortex

Glomerulus

Nephron

Renal Pyramid

Collecting Duct

* Say it like this:

"nef-ron"

"gluh-mair-you-luss"

The journey of wastes from bloodstream to urine starts in the cortex, in a ball of tiny blood vessels (capillaries) called the glomerulus* which has small holes for filtration. Water and waste pass through these holes, but larger materials like blood cells stay behind in the bloodstream. The liquid leaves the glomerulus and flows on to the nephron, where nutrients, chemicals, and water that you want to keep in your body

are reabsorbed (sucked back in). When the liquid arrives in the collecting duct, your body decides how much more water it wants to keep. In fact, only 1% of this liquid ends up becoming urine!

If you haven't been drinking much water, the collecting duct reabsorbs more water back into the body, and the urine that you excrete has a darker yellow color.

Fennec foxes have such efficient kidneys that they don't even need to drink water. Crocodiles, on the other hand, can't concentrate liquid at all, so their kidneys make solid waste to save water.

Straws and Balloons

Once the urine is in your kidney's collecting ducts, you need to get that waste out of your body. To prevent you from constantly peeing your pants, the rest of your renal system has a way of storing urine until you can find a bathroom.

The urine travels through special tubes called ureters - each kidney has 1, and each is like a long straw (8-10 inches long) with muscles that help push the urine along. At the ends of the tubes, the urine drops into the urinary bladder, which is kind of like a balloon surrounded by muscle. When urine fills the bladder, it can expand to up to 15 times its resting size until it holds up to 2 cups of urine. Because you make between 4 and 5 cups of urine a day, you need to empty the urinary bladder several times every day.

* Say it like this:

"your-eh-ter"

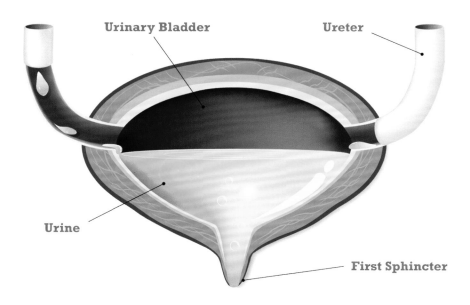

Urinary Bladder

Ureter

Urine

First Sphincter

When your kidneys are healthy, you make at least 1 tablespoon of urine an hour. So even when you are sleeping and not drinking water, you still produce urine.

Urine Trouble (But You'll Pee Alright)

As your urinary bladder fills up, it sends signals to your brain to tell you that you need to 'go.' That feeling is actually your body holding the urine inside your bladder by squeezing a sphincter*. Sphincters are rings of muscle that control the opening and closing of tubes in your body, such as the urethra.

When you pee, your body is sending urine from the bladder out through your urethra*, past the first sphincter. When this first sphincter opens, urine travels down the urethra until it reaches the final gate, the second sphincter. You control the opening or closing of this sphincter, which is why you can "hold your pee" until you find a toilet.

*Say it like this:

"sfink-ter"
"you-ree-thruh"

Just because you CAN "hold your pee" does not mean you SHOULD hold it for too long! Keeping a lot of urine in your bladder for a long time can lead to infections. Urine sitting around is a great place for bacteria to grow. When you start doing "the pee dance," you are trying to distract your bladder muscles from squeezing out urine. This means that you have been holding your urine for too long and should go to the bathroom right away!

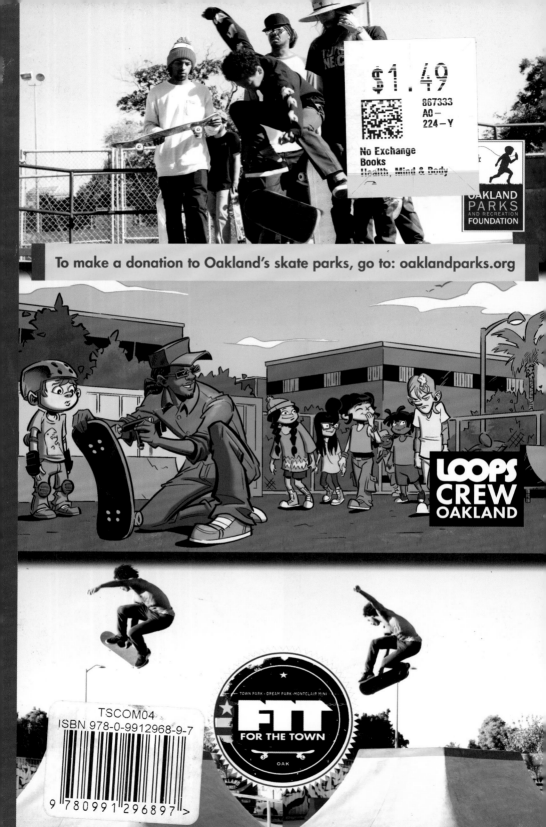

OAKLAND PARKS AND RECREATION FOUNDATION

To make a donation to Oakland's skate parks, go to: oaklandparks.org

LOOPS CREW OAKLAND

FTT
FOR THE TOWN
TOWN PARK · DREAM PARK · MONTCLAIR MINI
OAK